MATTESON PUBLIC LIBRARY

P9-CRI-909

Matteson Public Library

801 S. School Ave.

Matteson, IL 60443

Ph: 708-748-4431

www.mattesonpubliclibrary.org

BL 2.4 AR 0.5 = 1/2 pt

DEMCO

With love to my sister, Sindy, and her wonderful family—
Kurt, Laura, Sarah, and Kelly. You are such gifts to me!
—L.M.

For the perfect Lucy
—B.M.

Text copyright © 2010 by Lisa Moser
Illustrations copyright © 2010 by Ben Mantle

All rights reserved. Published in the United States by Random House Children's Books,
a division of Random House, Inc., New York.

Random House and the colophon are registered trademarks of Random House, Inc.

Visit us on the Web! www.randomhouse.com/kids

Educators and librarians, for a variety of teaching tools, visit us at www.randomhouse.com/teachers

Library of Congress Cataloging-in-Publication Data
Moser, Lisa.
Perfect Soup / by Lisa Moser ; illustrated by Ben Mantle. — 1st ed.
p. cm.
Summary: Murray the mouse goes into town for the carrot he needs to make Perfect Soup, and soon finds himself
with a chain of favors that will work only if a friendly snowman can help him get things started.
ISBN 978-0-375-86014-0 (trade) — ISBN 978-0-375-96014-7 (lib. bdg.)
[1. Soups—Fiction. 2. Snowmen—Fiction. 3. Mice—Fiction.] I. Mantle, Ben, ill. II. Title.
PZ7.M84696Per 2010
[E]—dc22
2009052846

MANUFACTURED IN CHINA

10 9 8 7 6 5 4 3 2 1

First Edition

Random House Children's Books supports the First Amendment and celebrates the right to read.

Perfect Soup

by Lisa Moser

illustrated by Ben Mantle

Random House   New York

MATTESON PUBLIC LIBRARY

Murray shined the teapot.
"Perfect," he said.

Murray set the table.
"Perfect."

Murray looked out the window.
"Soup is perfect on a snowy day."

He filled a pot with water and opened the cookbook.
"Ahhh. The recipe for Perfect Soup."

"Potatoes," read Murray.
Plop. Plop.

"Tomatoes," read Murray.
Plop. Plop. Plop.

"Corn," read Murray.
Plop. Plop. Plippety. Plop.

"Carrot," read Murray. No plop.
No plop at all.

Murray dashed around the kitchen and opened
all the cupboards. "No carrot," moaned Murray.
He put on his mittens and went outside.

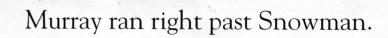

Murray ran right past Snowman.

Murray was in a hurry.

"Farmer, will you please give me a carrot?"
asked Murray. "I need a carrot for Perfect Soup."
Farmer leaned on his pitchfork. "I reckon I'd
give you a carrot if you hauled some logs from
the timber. I need wood to build a barn."

Murray thought about his soup.
He liked things perfect. "You will have
your wood!" said Murray.

Murray scurried through the meadow. Snowman smiled at him, but Murray didn't have time to stop. Murray was in a hurry.

"Horse, will you please haul some logs?
Farmer needs wood to build a barn.
And I need a carrot for Perfect Soup."
Horse shook her mane and whinnied. "I'll caaarrry
those logs if you give me jingle bells. I want to be
faaancy like the town horses."
Murray bit his lip. Perfect Soup had potatoes,
tomatoes, corn and carrot. "I think I can get some
jingle bells," said Murray.

Murray walked into town. Snowman waved one stick arm, but Murray didn't have time to wave back.

Murray was in a hurry.

"Shopkeeper, will you please give me your bells?
Horse needs bells to feel fancy.
Farmer needs wood to build a barn.
And I need a carrot for Perfect Soup."
Shopkeeper peered over his spectacles. "I'll trade
some jingle bells if you shovel my walk."

Murray looked at the mountain of snow and the shovel he couldn't even lift. He tugged on his whiskers and twisted his tail. "Maybe I can find someone to shovel your walk," he squeaked.

Murray climbed the hill. Snowman wrote
a message in the snow, but Murray didn't
have time to look.

Murray was in a hurry.

"Miller's Boy, will you please shovel a walk?
Shopkeeper needs a nice, clean walk.
Horse needs bells to feel fancy.
Farmer needs wood to build a barn.

And I need a carrot
for Perfect Soup."

Miller's Boy poked a finger through a hole in his mitten.
"I would shovel a walk if I had new mittens."
Murray flopped in the snow. He needed that carrot.
If he didn't have the carrot, his soup wouldn't be perfect.
"There's a teeny-weeny chance I could get a pair of mittens."

Murray plodded down the road.
Snowman called out, "Stay and play!"

Murray shook his head. He didn't have
time to play. He needed things to be perfect.
Murray was in a hurry.

"Mrs. Wooley, will you please knit some mittens?
Miller's Boy needs mittens for his cold, cold hands.
Shopkeeper needs a nice, clean walk.
Horse needs bells to feel fancy.
Farmer needs wood to build a barn.
And I need a carrot for Perfect Soup."

Mrs. Wooley shook her finger at Murray.
"Accchhh! Such a bad, bad day. My yarn is
a jumble. My cocoa just burned my tongue.
I will not knit mittens on this bad, bad day."
And with that, she slammed the door on Murray.

Murray trudged home, sat down and cried.

"What's wrong?" asked a voice.

Murray looked around. He saw Snowman.

"Cocoa burned Mrs. Wooley's mouth. And I will never have Perfect Soup," Murray said with a sob.

"I can help," said Snowman. He reached up and scooped a bit of snow off a tree branch.

Then he plopped the snow into Murray's lap. "That will cool the cocoa."

Murray sighed. "But what do you want for helping me?" he asked.

"Nothing," said Snowman. "It's a gift."

"A gift?" whispered Murray. "For me?" He jumped up. He ran over to Snowman and hugged him. "Thank you!"

Murray ran all the way back to Mrs. Wooley's house.

He plopped the snow
into her cocoa.

He sorted yarns and wound
them into bright balls.

Mrs. Wooley took a long drink. "This is good cocoa. This is neat yarn. You have turned this into a good day to knit." She knitted a pair of mittens.

"These mittens are warm," said Miller's Boy.
He shoveled the walk.

"This walk is clean and clear," said Shopkeeper.
He wrapped up the bells.

"These bells make me feel faaancy," said Horse.
She hauled the logs.

"This wood will make a fine barn," said Farmer.
He gave a carrot to Murray.

Murray whistled while he finally finished cooking his soup.

He put on his mittens and went outside.

Murray ate soup with his new friend.
It did not have a carrot.
It was perfect.

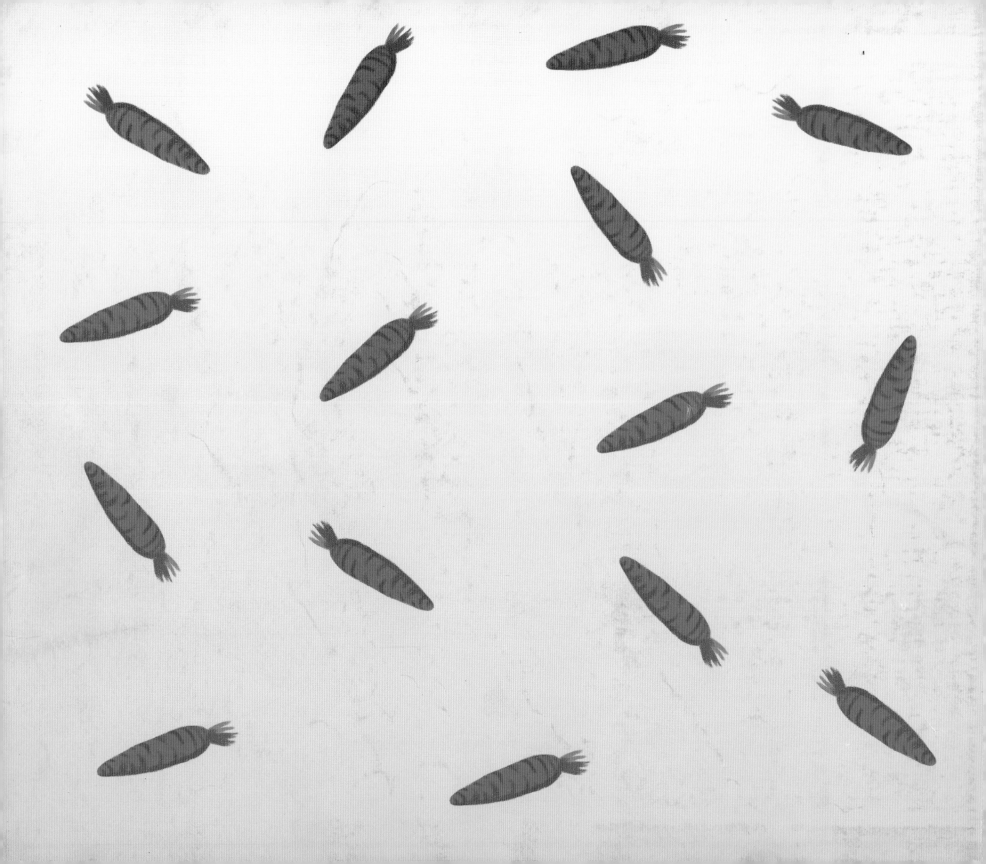